SHORT STORIES

Tales of Madness

Michael Gregory II

Short Stories

All short stories were inspired from story prompts from :
https://blog.reedsy.com/creative-writing-prompts
For information contact :
mikegreg85@outlook.com
http://www.beacons.ai/mikegregory
ISBN: 9798844105883
First Edition: August 2022

CONTENTS

The Dark Room

What's that noise? What is that? The buzzing, inconsistent buzzing. It sounds like a flickering light, where is that coming from? I can't see anything, its pitch black, darker than the large pupils of my eyes from not being able to see. Its nothingness, absolute blank. Where am I? How did I get here? I don't understand any of this. Why is this happening to me? Ok, if I am going to attempt to do anything I guess I will follow that sound and hope it leads me somewhere I want to be.

Reach out, I don't feel anything, there has to be a wall or something, right? Ok, still nothing, my head is killing me, what is this place? Fuck, I just rammed my shin into something that felt like an edge of a wooden crate. Great, I am bleeding from my shin now. I can feel the warmth of the crimson liquid as it flows down my leg soaking into my pant leg and saturating my sock all the way into my shoe. How was a crate so sharp? I was moving so slowly. Wait, where did the crate go? It's gone, like it grew legs and moved away on its own without making a peep.

Focus, try to follow the noise. Be slow, hold your hands out, glide your feet so you don't get injured again. This shit hurts, I'm pretty sure I am leaving a trail of blood now. What was that? It sounded like there was something moving in the distance. What do I do? Do I ask if someone's there? What if they are the ones who moved the crate? Fuck, what the fuck do I do? Ok, let's ask and hope someone is there. "Hello? is there anyone there? I hurt myself and can't find my way out of here. Where ever here even is." No answer. What do I do? Just keep going, I guess. The noise is getting louder so I assume I am getting closer, I hope.

What was that? Scratching on the floor of what seems to be 20 feet behind me. Shit, that sounds sharp whatever that is. I don't want to find out what that is. Shuffle faster, move quicker. Why does it seem like I am moving but going nowhere? I don't understand anything that is going on. The flickering is getting louder finally. Ok, what is this? I think I just found a wall. Great, it's a wall, there's no door here. What do I do? Feel the wall, see if there is a door somewhere. The flickering is on the other side of the wall in front of me. Where would a door be?

Maybe to the left, ok, follow with your hands and move to the left.

Wham, something big just slammed against the wall next to me. What the fuck was that? It sounded heavy and solid, that's not good. Wham, that time it hit to the left side of me clipping my fingers I can't scream I know my pinky and ring finger are broken. Don't show your hurt, focus on the wall. There, I feel a door frame, yes! Find the door knob, there it is, twist and pull. Shit, I need to push the door open, twist the knob again and now to push...smack, a crate smashes into my back knocking me through the door into the room with the flickering light.

I can't breathe, can I walk? Can I get up? What threw that? Slowly I roll onto my back as I am in agony, breathless, but cognitive enough to know that what threw that had ill intentions and will probably be following up on its target soon. I don't like that the target was me so I need to try to move. Sitting up I look past the doorway into a room that looks like it has been abandoned off of the earth and only exists in the realm of nothingness. There is no light in there, not even when it flickers in this room. Pull my feet through and slam it shut, hurry, before the beast gets through.

Ok, feet through, need to close the door now. What's that noise? it's the scratching, oh shit, fuck, now it's screeching like some sort of demonic bat cry searching for blood. I think it's moving towards me, fuck, it's moving fast. Slam the door, fast, hurry, stand up. Ok doors closed, whack, I think it threw another big crate, I am glad I closed the door this time. I'm fucked up. Everything hurts. Ok, focus, where is the light. It's across the room, in a corner next to a door. Let's move there, hopefully that thing can't open that door. What was it anyway? Ok, I can't walk, I am going to attempt to crawl there, let's move.

Boom, something bigger hit the door behind me.

Oh no, whatever that is has hit the door. I guess it doesn't know how to turn a knob. Boom, again, this time harder, the door doesn't seem like it's going to last so I better hurry. Crawling closer to the light I hear a voice, faintly, I can't make out what it is saying though. I yell out to it "HELP ME something is trying to kill me!" No answer, even after shouting many times. It's up to you to get there yourself and get through that door. Wait, the door, what is it doing? It seems to be opening and closing with the slightest crack. Just a small ray of light peers in when it does. Oddly enough, every time I hear the voice the crack follows shortly after. Wait, in-between the voice and the door cracking the light is flickering and making the noise.

Bam, one last time and the door flics open. I feel my heart sink into my stomach as I know I can't move fast and that thing has bad intentions with me. Look back, fuck what is that? Oh...my....God... It's huge, full of muscle, blank face, big black eyes, pale skin, long fingers, sharp claws, oh no, huge sharp teeth. It's screeching again. It's not looking at me, what is it doing? Keep crawling, silently, please don't notice me. It's sniffing the air, oh no, it looks right at me. It opens its mouth, what's it doing? Grabbing a tooth and pulling it out? Why? Throws the tooth, stabs me in my leg, not the one that was bleeding already, now both bleeding and in serious pain. What am I doing here? What did I do to deserve this? Ok, focus, where are you going? To the door next to the flickering light, keep moving. I hear the sound again; it gets louder as I get closer.

The beast starts walking slowly to me. I better hurry. It's pulling another tooth, fuck. It lands in my left hand, impaling it to the ground and pinning me there. I pull my hand out over the top all the way through. Ok, move, fast. I get closer to the noise; it sounds like someone saying "clear." That's odd, what does it mean? I look back and it's hunting me, watching me as I go. It's catching up, fuck. Ok, fuck it, stand up, run, who cares how much this hurts, that thing wants to suck the life out of you. I am running, oh no it is running, its fast. How big is this room? Are we even moving? Ok, almost there. The voice is saying clear, then the loud light now is buzzing and there is the door light cracking. Ok I'm at the door, its locked, fuck, what do I do? Look back, there it is, closing in, 10 feet, 5 feet, 3 feet... Clear, buzzing noise, door cracked, pushed open and through to the light...

I open my eyes; I am on a table. I look around at the bright lights, there are people. What just happened? Where am I? what was that thing? Wait they are talking, wait, they are doctors. My shirt is cut open. What is this? The doctor says "sir, say something, can you hear me? How do you feel?" I look at him and say, "where am I?" He replies "you are at the ER. You had a heart attack and were flatlined for 2 minutes. You are lucky that the defibrillator was able to bring you back to life."

Short Stories

A Night in Paris

s this a déjà vu? This can't be real, can it? I don't even understand what the hell is even going on. Why is everyone looking at me like that? Ok, this doesn't make any sense at all. Ok, think Jack, why are you here. Wait, where is here? How can I figure out why I am here when I don't even know where here is? Shit, this is going to be harder than I thought. Look around but don't make eye contact. Who is this beautiful blonde woman walking my direction while looking at me? Don't panic, she's getting closer, ok now she's approaching. The mysterious blonde woman says "Jack, are you ok? You look a little flushed."

I wake up to my alarm buzzing. 06:00 AM, ok time to get up and get the day started. Get out of bed, stretch, take some deep breaths, drink an iced cold cup of water. Wait, I'm in a hotel. I don't remember why I am here, am I hungover? I don't feel like I am hungover. Go look out the window, wow, the Eiffel Tower, I'm in France. I didn't expect that, why am I in France? Go take a shower, maybe it will come back to you.

So refreshed, a shower in the morning like that feels amazing. That shower has water spraying in every direction, steam from the floor, I felt like I was being washed in a dishwasher set to human cycle with a steam finish. What do I have to wear? Let's check the dresser drawers. Top drawer, good we got black socks, blue boxer briefs, perfect. Second row drawer, we've got blue jeans, lucky brand, and a nice white t-shirt which is John Varvatos. I'm happy I have good taste. Focus, brush teeth, put on deodorant, spray cologne, put some sculpting creme in my hair then brush it, part it on the left.

Look around the room now for some clues to why I might be in France. What's the last thing you remember now Jack? I remember a gorgeous blonde woman who was talking to me and knew me. Who was she? What happened after that? Was I here with her? Why do I not remember who she is? Ok Jack, you're getting distracted, let's look around. She's not here right now, let's check the other drawers and see if there are other clothes. No, only what appears to be mine. There's a table, anything on it? Yes, a note, what does it say? "Jack, meet me for dinner at Frame Brasserie, 8 PM don't be late. XOXO A" There's a start, who is A? How do I know her? Why am I in Paris?

What time is it now? I am getting a little hungry, let's see what's inside the hotel. Looks like I'm on the top floor, looks like the 7th floor to be exact. Ding, door opens, step out, look around and the man at the front desk is looking at me and smiles. "Monsieur Jack, how was your sleep? Have a good day and enjoy Paris." I just look and nod my head with a quick "wonderful, thank you." Let's move swiftly out the door before he tries to make conversation. Next step, coffee.

There, a little cafe. "Hi, can I get a table outside?" The hostess replies "of course monsieur, are you expecting company again?" I confusingly respond "nope, just me thanks." Ok, everyone seems to know me, this is getting weirder. Order a latte, and a couple croissants. Why didn't I think about checking my phone, I know there has to be clues there? Setting the phone on the table, turn it on, unlock code....wait, what's the code? Let's try this 4 5 8 7, no. Birth year 1 9 7 7, no. Month and day 0 3 1 7, no, shit now it's locked. There goes that idea.

A man sits at my table in front of me and staring at me blankly. "Can I help you?" I ask. He responds

"Jack, you're in danger, pay your bill and meet me outside. Make it fast there isn't much time." He immediately gets up and runs off while saying loudly "my mistake, sorry monsieur."

I am already confused and scared at this point but what happens next was even more unpredictable. I see two large men, both in suits, stand up from the table in the corner and start walking towards me. Worried now, I drop money on the table, not even sure if it's enough but I get up and start to walk away. I look back, they never even take their eye sight away from me. Shit, what is this? What do I do? Why are they coming for me? A waiter walks in front of them, they don't stop and knock them down. Now I know they mean business and I start running and get out the door. The man who sat at my table pulls up on a Vespa scooter and says "hop on." I yell at him "who are you and who are they?" He replies "get on otherwise you will find out who they are but not how you would want to." I hear commotion behind me and I jump on the Vespa, he takes off as fast as possible. I look back and one is running after us, the other I see pull up behind the runner and stops for him to jump on. We are now in a full-on chase; how did I get here?

I yell to the man driving "they are right behind us, hurry up!" He looks back and I can see the fear in his eyes but he says nothing. "That's not good" I said to myself. He's zooming around, it appears he really knows these streets. I look back and apparently, they know them too because they haven't missed a beat. Then I hear a loud BANG, POP. Our Vespa back tire was shot by the men. We lose control and slide sideways. My jeans and shirt are getting scuffed and torn from sliding on the ground and we hit a food cart. Everything is flying everywhere. I am hurt. My whole side hurts. I don't want to know what these guys want from me. I get up and the man who was driving screams to me "GET OUT OF HERE JACK!" I don't look back, I just run. There it is, the Eiffel Tower. Surely there would be police or someone to help me. I'm sure they won't follow me there. Limping my way as fast as I can I hear a loud bang followed by lots of commotion behind me. I glance back at what appears to be the men had gotten off their Vespa. One is holding a gun and standing above what looks like the now limp man that drove me here. The other looked at me and started running, fuck, what do I do?

There, I see a police man in the distance, get to him, quickly. "Sir, there are two men chasing me, I don't know why, and I am pretty sure they just killed some man over there." He doesn't say anything, he just looks at me, then he peaks his head over my shoulder and BANG. One of the men chasing me shoot the police man in the head. He grabs me by the shirt and says "not so fast Jack. She's waiting for you." "Who is she? What does she want from me? Is it the blonde I remember?" He doesn't answer, he just walks me to a black car that is idling in the street. He throws me in the back, gets in beside me and another man is in the front. They drive off.

I look at them and ask "what is this all about? I

don't understand any of this?" No answer. I guess I will just have to wait and see. The throbbing starts after a while. I completely forgot I slid across the ground and am cut up on my left side. "I think I need a doctor" I tell them, "No thanks to you I took a horrific tumble back there." No response besides a half grin from the man sitting next to me.

We pull up to a building, wait, is that Frame Brasserie? That's where the note said to meet. They drag me across the street to what looks like an unmarked building. They open the door, there's a lot of people in here. What is this? It looks like some sort of fancy fashion store with a lounge and pretty much anything you could ask for. He pushes me to a couch; I look up and, on the wall, there is an "A" and it distinctly looks like the one that was written on the note in my room. A doctor comes up to me, checks me out, cleans my wounds and patches me up where necessary. He didn't say a word. Next, some sort of tailor walks up, stands me up, measures me and walks off.

Why is no one talking, everyone is busy but not a word from anyone. A waiter comes up to me and hands me a drink, it's a good bourbon, neat. Well, might as well enjoy it while I can and drink it fast. Another delivered instantly. Two women come up to me and pull me towards a room, they take me inside and show me to the bathroom which oddly looks like the one I stayed in. I take a shower, the women stay outside of the bathroom, is there a window? Can I escape? Of course, there is no window. What time is it? Oh wait, I still have my phone, I can call the police. I grab my clothes and pull out the phone, shit, its broken. It must've broken when I fell on the Vespa. I put on a robe on that was hanging by the shower then enter the room. There is a suit laid out for me. Very classy, something I would want to wear in different circumstances. I put it on being there is nothing else to wear. I surprisingly feel really good, my wounds don't even bother me, maybe it's all the bourbon. "Keep'em coming waiter man" I yell out hoping he hears me. Sure enough there he is with another.

The big man says "it's ten to eight, it's time for your appointment." My heart starts beating fast and hard. I completely forgot about how the note said don't be late to meet at the restaurant across the street. We start walking across, I look around and am thinking I might be able to make a run for it. The big man grabs my shoulder and just shakes his head. There goes that idea. He takes me in, the host looks at me and says "right this way to your table, have a seat right here and the madam will be here shortly."

I start to look around but don't make eye contact. There she is, who is this beautiful blonde woman walking my direction while looking at me? Don't panic, she's getting closer, ok now she's approaching. She says "Hi Jack, I know you must be confused. My name is Abigail. You are in a special place. You died, you were on vacation in Paris and you had a terrible accident on your Vespa. The problem is, you were not a good person when you were alive. Now I have your soul, this is where you

22

will spend eternity. Doing this over and over. This is purgatory." Then the mysterious blonde woman says "Jack, are you ok? You look a little flushed." I wake up to my alarm buzzing. 06:00 AM.

False Hope

Praise the Lord Baby Jesus!" screamed Father John. "Betty Sue, I command you to be healed." The entire building erupts and starts chanting "Betty Sue, Betty Sue, Betty Sue." Father John then starts jumping around and speaking in tongues. In reality it sounds more like a two-year-old who is just learning to speak and gets excited rambling gibberish at the fastest rate their little mush mouth allows them to. Father John is getting so wild that he has the appearance of a fish flopping on the ground. He is drenched in sweat so it fits the aquatic narrative perfectly. Now Father John stops abruptly, and speaks quietly to everyone in the crowd "it's time, quiet down everyone. It is time for you, Betty Sue. It is time for you to step up out of that wheel chair. Time for your legs to work as they were intended to by our Lord and saviour. Stand up, you are healed."

Silence has taken over the entire building that you could hear the sweat drops as they fall from Father Johns brow and drip on the concrete floor below him. All eyes were now on Betty Sue. She has a new found look of confidence, determination. Slowly she grabs her wheel chair brake on the side, sets to lock. Puts her hands onto the arm rests and looks down to her legs. She grabs one with her hands and puts it to the floor, then she does the same with the other. Betty Sue then lets out a raspy excitable grunt and pushes herself up on to her feet. Now standing, she looks to Father John and yells "I am healed!" then immediately starts walking towards

Father John.

Father John then stands there with a grin wider than a freshly carved jack o lantern as Betty Sue reaches him and hugs him tightly with tears flowing from her eyes. Father John then asks "Betty Sue, how long has it been since you've been able to use those God given movement machines?" Betty Sue responds "I haven't been able to walk in twenty five years. Ever since I was ran over by a hit and run driver. They hit me and left me to die in a gutter. But now I am fully healed thanks to you Father John." He replies "Don't thank me, thank our Lord, he works in mysterious ways. This was all a part of Gods plan. From the accident that harmed you, to bringing his power to you in front of all of these holy people to prove that faith is stronger than anything."

The entire crowd is in amazement, people are screaming, falling over to the ground crying in disbelief. A woman in the front row shrieked " OH MY GOD, my Lord and savior healed this beautiful woman Betty Sue in front of our eyes! I cannot believe it, actually yes, I can. Faith heals us all!" Father John calmly walked over to his podium and looked around, then said "Imagine that everyone, a miracle has happened right before your eyes. Can you believe it? We just witnessed a woman's life change significantly, all with the power of faith in our Lord. Hallelujah, this has taken quite a bit out of me though and I will need to return to my dwellings to get some rest. Thank you everyone, and let's get the collection plates moving around so I can continue to travel around the world and help spread our Lords amazing power to heal with faith. God bless you all, none of this could be done without you. Only give what you can, most tend to do ten percent of their annual salary, but do what you can." Betty Sue was now walking around and talking with many others who are all still in disbelief. At this time Father John waved his good byes and went behind the curtains to walk to his bus.

Father John walked into the back of the bus where his bed is, threw off his jacket to the chair in the corner. He kicked off his boots to the other side of the bus. He then jumped onto his bed and grabbed the big bottle of Jack Daniels that was sitting on the side table next to his bed. Takes a big swig and lets out a big sigh of relief then says "now that's the real miracle, bourbon is my faith healer". Father John continues to drink until he feels as if his own miracle is performed for himself to be able to get up and go to the bathroom where he gets into the shower. Realizing he forgot to urinate prior to getting in the shower he says "fuck it" to himself and relieves himself in the shower while still taking swigs from his half empty bottle. Getting out of the shower he lazily half way dry's himself off and proceeds to get to his bed where he falls down onto without getting dressed and passes out.

"Rise and shine" Father John wakes to a familiar voice speaking to him. Lifting his head out of the puddle of his slumber drool, he looks over and see's Betty Sue sitting in the chair. "How did we do? You really sold it well this go round." He responded.

Betty Sue says "First put some pants on, I don't need to see your little pecker standing at attention while I am talking to you." Father John laughs and says "Ok, ok. How much did we make and how long will it take for us to get to the next town?" Father John proceeds to put on his pants and then grabs his bottle of whiskey and takes a swig. "Breakfast of champions." Father John mumbled. Betty Sue replied "We made sixty five thousand on this one. Hey John, don't you ever feel bad that we are taking advantage of all these people week after week? We make them think I am being healed, but our whole crew knows it's a sham but we're getting rich so they don't complain." Father John responds "Betty Sue, now don't you go getting soft on me. We are all in this together. You may not be getting healed week after week but we provide these people a service. A service of absolute belief in their faith and that is something that is worth paying for." Betty Sue says "I know, I just wonder if they ever realize later on that I don't actually live in their town and that they had been hosed." Father John replies "I understand but this is all a part of Gods plan." Father John then takes a big swig of his bottle then turns to Betty Sue. When they make eye contact, they both laugh uncontrollably as they ensue to the next   town.

Break of Dawn

As I am looking out the window and realizing that dawn is upon us. I yell to Cynthia neurotically "we're running out of time." It was at that moment I knew we were fucked. Cynthia turned and had a look in her eyes as if she had seen a hand breaking through the ground to pull me to hell.

"Shit, shit, shit. What are we going to do Xander? We need to find somewhere to hide."

Cynthia responded frantically.

I worryingly respond, "Let me think. Fuck. Ok. Over there, it looks like an abandoned warehouse by the dock. Hopefully they have a basement or somewhere we can block out the light."

"Ok, good idea. I hope they don't find us in there though. We'll be trapped."

"At this point we don't have a choice. It's either the sun or the hunters."

I run as fast as the speed of sound, or what seems to be that fast, to the abandoned warehouse. The building is built out of tin. I don't see any windows, that's fantastic. The door is at the end of the building, right by the dock, it's locked. Luckily, I am as strong as a giant pissed off silverback gorilla and can turn the handle and break the lock. I'm in, I look over and Cynthia comes flying in as well. I scan the room and I see stairs.

"Over there, down the stairs." I firmly suggest.

"Works for me." Cynthia responds slightly relieved.

Even though it has only been two minutes since we were outside, it feels as if it has been an entire lifetime ago. We get to the bottom of the stairs and realize that this might be the worst place we could possibly hide. There is a giant opening of a wall that leads to the ocean. Fortunately, in the middle of the dock is a boat suspended on ropes and covered with thick tarps.

"We don't have time." I told Cynthia, "Looks like we will be resting in the boat."

Both of us jump into the boat pull the tarps back and triple check to make sure no light can get in. We are safe, from the sun at least.

"Those fanger's are fast, aren't they?" Thomas yelled to Billy and Jason. "It's dawn now, so they either found a place to hide or they burnt up in the sunlight. Either way these devils will be dragged back to hell today where they belong."

Thomas, Billy, and Jason were the best vampire hunters since Van Helsing. Or at least they like to think of themselves that way. Following a trail of blood drops from one of the vampires they had shot with a silver bullet, this keeps the wound from healing fast like it would with any ordinary weapon. The only thing was tracking the blood drops took a keen eye. They were moving so fast that the blood drops were separated about fifty feet from each other.

"Over here, this way." Jason yelled to the others while pointing down an alley way.

"Dumb bastards." Billy said, "They couldn't have made it any easier to follow."

The three hunters walk at a steady pace down the alley while all keeping their eyes to the ground looking for the next droplet. They all notice the next at the same time and simultaneously smile. Through the alley way they get to an open industrial corridor where there are many buildings. Thomas looks at Billy and Jason then puts his finger up to his dried split lips and shushes them. He then points to Billy, then points to the left signaling where he wants him to investigate. Next, he points to Jason, then points to the right. Knowing that they are getting close, they all move quietly.

At this point, there was no more blood droplets to be found. The wound had healed since the last drop in the alley. The hunters realized this won't be as easy as they thought it was going to be. They are going to have to search and investigate each building. Thomas waived his arms to get the attention of Billy and Jason, then signaled them to all meet in the middle of the corridor.

Thomas whispered, "Ok guys, we need to figure out what we want to do. They are in one of these buildings, no doubt. But if they are together in a dark room, no way one of us can take them on alone. It's more time consuming but I think we need to check them all together."

Billy and Jason looked at each other, then both turned to Thomas and nodded their heads nervously.

The three of them creep toward the building on the right across the corridor. Most of the buildings are two stories high, some are three. In the buildings that are two stories there is five to seven office rooms. There are also big open rooms on each floor that have many tables and chairs for what looks like meeting rooms for presentations. There is also a men's and women's bathroom with several stalls on each floor. The two story buildings take them a little over an hour to cover from top to bottom. The three story buildings take them just over an hour and a half. There are a total of nine buildings, four of which are three stories and five that are two stories including the abandoned warehouse by the dock in the upper left corner of the corridor. The team is zig zagging back and forth from the right to left covering each building till the reach the upper right corner and will only move to the left at that point.

I look at my phone after waking and see that we

have been here for nine hours now. Well at least we are still alive and haven't been found. Checking now on my weather app I see that we have maybe two hours till dusk. I focus my hearing in which I can listen a great distance, being a vampire has its perks. I hear the hunters, damn, they are still searching for us. It sounds as if they are around three buildings down. We don't want to hurt them, hell we don't want to hurt anyone. Little do these hunters know that we are evolved We take blood from blood banks. We don't kill anyone; we don't even feed off of anyone directly. We are lovers, we just want to live in peace. There are traditional vamps everywhere that give us a bad rap with society. We generally try to stay hidden, but if the other vamps are in town we will get sought out and have to move or get killed when hunters are employed.

I look at Cynthia and grab her hand and give it a gentle squeeze. I whisper to her "dusk is almost here. As soon as the suns down we will get to the next town. We'll figure out a new place to get to and start over again." I give her a half smile knowing that this is not an easy task. Surviving the rest of the day is not guaranteed to begin with. She smiles back with her eyes tearing up. She doesn't say anything, she doesn't have to. I know what she's feeling, I can sense her distraught. All I can do is comfort her and hold her while being stranded in this tarp covered damp boat and pray we will live to see another night.

Thomas, Billy, and Jason have now reached the last building which is the abandoned warehouse by the dock. Thomas mumbles "We at the last one, either they in there or they dead already. Either way be ready, the sun is coming down quick. We probably have twenty minutes till dusk." Billy and Jason just nod. The hunters don't say it to each other but they are all feeling fatigued at this point. They have been chasing the vampires for almost twenty four hours straight with no sleep. The anxiety and deliria are really starting to set in from the lack of sleep and knowing that this is do or die, right here, right now.

Thomas gets to the door and notices that the handle has been crushed. He gets a huge smile on his face and shows his comrades. "It's fucking go time." Thomas murmurs excitedly. They open the door and slowly start stalking the building in a formation that appears to be military like with guns drawn. They are packing all silver bullets and have wooden stakes inside their jackets where custom holsters have been sewn in. This is an abandoned warehouse so there is much less to look through. One office, clear. Second office, clear. Third office, clear. Adrenaline is now pumping through their veins, each heartbeat adding an extra surge of excitement as they slowly cover the building. Top floor, clear. Time to move to the bottom floor which is where the personal dock of the warehouse resides.

I am watching my phone clock; the seconds feel

as if it's an hour between each tick. I can hear the hunters; they are in the building. They are making their way to the stairs which will lead them to us. There are very few spots for them to look down here so they will naturally look in the boat first thing. Each footstep down the stairs is as loud and clear as if the soles in their boots were steel and they were stomping on a wood floor. Thump. Thump. Thump. I put my phone away knowing this is it, there is no turning back.

I grab Cynthia's hand tighter as I see the corner of the tarp start to lift. Without hesitation I grab the barrel of the rifle that started to point in. With brute strength I bent the barrel upwards and throw it at one of the other hunters and knock him down. I grab and throw the hunter in front of me against a wall knocking the wind out of him. Cynthia screams, "Watch out!" I hear the gun go off. I was shot in the shoulder by the last hunter on the stairs. I am pissed off now, I run to him and headbutt him in the nose. Blood flies as if a water balloon filled with red liquid and splattered all over his and my face. I can taste the warm and delicious delicacy. O positive, but he has high cholesterol.

The hunter falls on the stairs wailing in agony while holding his decimated nose. I bellow to Cynthia, "Go go go, here's our chance." She runs, faster than I've ever seen her move. Up the stairs, I start to follow and bang. Shot again, this time in the leg. Bang, the other leg. I let out a roar of despair. Its slowing me down but I signal to Cynthia to keep going, she doesn't. I make it to the top of the stairs when I look back and see the other two hunters running after us. They point their rifles at us, I push Cynthia out of the way, bang, bang. Both hit me in the chest. I am laid out on the ground.

Thomas and Billy run up the stairs knowing they had taken down the male vampire. Jason passed out from the pain or blood loss from his what used to be a nose. Thomas looks at Billy and dictates, "You keep an eye for the female, this mother fucker is mine to stake." Without hesitation Billy runs to the top of the stairs and points his gun around searching for his target. Thomas gets to the top of the stairs shortly after Billy and hovers over the male vampire. Smirking, he opens his jacket and pulls out a stake and stabs it into the vampires left hand. He pulls out another, then slams it to the right. He then proceeds to repeat this to both feet.

Thomas says proudly, "Time to die blood suck—"

The female vampire grabs one of Thomas' stakes out of his jacket and stabs it in the side of his neck then pulls it out in the blink of an eye. Blood sprays out as if someone just ran over a fire hydrant. Billy screams and starts shooting as fast as he can at the female vampire. He hits her in the stomach, arms, and shoulders several times. On her way down she throws the stake with a trail of blood flying in the air which pummels into Billy's shoulder. They both collapse as if they were in a synchronized dance finale.

===

Cynthia crawls to me, I can see she is hurt.

I beg, "My love, please remove these stakes from me. I will get us out of here."

She whimpers, "Please forgive me."

As she rips them out of me, I let out a howl that would frighten King Kong. This alarmed the last conscious hunter who was trying to get to his feet. Even though he has a stake in his shoulder, he gets up pulls out a stake from his jacket and starts to stumble in our direction. I can't quite stand up yet, there is too much pain. I roll in his direction and he jumps while screaming with the stake raised above his head. He comes down driving it at me, I quickly put my hand up in which the stake drives through the hole that is already starting to heal. I roll him to my side and I do the unthinkable. I rip the stake out of my hand and start to feed on him.

I call Cynthia over, "We need to heal, lets drain him and go."

Reluctantly she drags herself over and starts to feed on his wrist while I feed on his neck. We are regaining our strength, regretting that we have to feed on a human, but this is survival. He is dead. We gather ourselves feeling ashamed and stand up like a pair of drunks trying to leave after last call. I look at Cynthia and smile, "We are free. Let's g—." I feel the wet soaking in the front of my shirt. I look at Cynthia and her white shirt is now red as she falls face first lifeless. Now the tunnel vison sets in as my conscious drains away and I glance back with one last look to see the hunter with the busted nose staring at me.

WHAT'S YOUR DESIRES?

Have you ever had the feeling that someone was watching you? It's not a feeling you can describe if you wanted to. It is just an inner knowing, as if there are invisible fingers that are flying from their eyes and gently grazing you, teasing you. When you quickly feel the area as if there is a bug crawling on you, yet there is nothing there. It's almost as if there is a heat signature left behind, but you just can't quite prove any of it happened or that there was anything at all. Only what I could describe as the feeling of devil eyes burning your skin. You quickly look around in a panic. Is there anyone looking at me? Will anyone lock eyes with me? Will I catch someone staring at me? Am I going crazy? At this point everyone is probably staring at me, who am I kidding. No one is looking at me, perfect. Time to just carry on.

I just got off of work, so maybe it's all the nerves of the day at the office that is making me feel uneasy. I am taking the bus, it's kind of uncomfortable as it is, right? There's a lot of people on here, I am sure someone was looking at me. This is probably just a big joke to them at this point. Ok, scan the bus, don't make it obvious. I am on the middle left of the bus, start with in front of you all the way to the driver. Slowly turn your head, no one is looking at you. Alright Richard, I think you are playing games with yourself. Look all the way behind you, ok no one is even paying attention. Wait, who is that? There he is, just staring at you. At the back of the bus, opposite side.

Maybe he's not looking at you, look around, is there someone or something else he could be looking at? Nope, he is definitely looking at me. I knew it. He's just staring, with a smile. Dressed very nice, in what seems to be some sort of designer suit, every bit of it black except the shirt is a deep red. He has neatly combed hair parted to the side, its black with a few grey streaks. Mustache and goatee perfectly groomed with what looks like a sharp point coming off of his chin. He has an eerie feeling about him, creepy. This is even more uncomfortable now that I noticed him. He won't take his eyes off of me even though he knows I know he's looking at me. I am going to get off at the next stop, I don't care, just nod, smile and look away. Here we are, next stop, perfect, right at the shopping center. I could really use going to Barnes and Noble. Grab a coffee and try to just relax and look at a magazine or something.

I didn't see him getting off of the bus, in fact I am sure I am the only one who got off. Man that was really weird, why was that guy just staring at me? Alright, let's get over this, first step Starbucks.

"Welcome to Starbucks, what can we get started for you?" asked the barista.

"Hi, can I please get a venti white chocolate mocha with almond milk? That will be it." I replied.

"Your total will be six dollars and thirty six cents; will that be cash or card? Can I get a name for the order?"

"I will pay with the app, thank you. My name is Richard."

"Thank you Richard, your order will be up shortly and called out over at that counter."

Time to find a magazine, how about classic cars, there is something relaxing about a nice American muscle car. Alright, now let's go find a table to sit down and relax.

"Richard, venti white chocolate mocha."

Perfect, I'll go grab my coffee and look at all these nice cars. Sit down, open up the magazine, wow! That is an amazing sixty-nine Pontiac GTO

Judge. Matte black, with matching matte black rims. So beautiful, what I would do to get one of those.

"What would you do for one of those?" A deep raspy voice says in front of me.

I look up and I see the man from the bus. This can't be! I'm in shock, I don't even know what to say.

I respond shakily, "What? Did you follow me off the bus? How did you get off the bus? Are you following me?"

"Never mind all that, I am Samael, but I just go by Lou to make it easy." He sits down at my table without asking and continues, "I saw you on the bus. I could tell there was something special about you. You have some deep desires and dreams. I am able to help you with them."

"What, what do you mean? Listen Lou, you are really starting to freak me out right now."

"Richard, stop. I promise, I will be able to fulfill every desire you've ever had."

"How did you know my name was Richard?

What do you mean you could fulfill every desire I've ever had?"

"I know everyone's name at a Starbucks. All you have to do is look at their name written down on their cup. Ha ha, or what if I told you I know everyone's name anywhere? Ok, I'll stop with that. Let's get down to business. What is your every desire? What is it you really want out of life? Nothing too big, nothing too weird."

"Ok Lou, I'll play along. Let's see, I want this car on the picture here. I want a big mansion. I want twenty million dollars in my bank account so I can quit my job. Oh yea, I want a beautiful wife who is so in love with me." At this point I have a huge grin on my face. There is no way he can fulfill any of this, right?

"That's its Richard? Easy, all you have to do is sign this paper, go home and go to sleep. When you wake up, your dream will be reality."

"What? Are you serious? What is this paper?" I look at the paper and realize I can't read it. "What does this say? I can't read it."

"It doesn't say much. It's more of a type of memento for me. See, I am capable of imaginable things and it makes me very happy to help others. All I ask is for a signature."

"Fuck it, I'll sign your paper, Lou. What's the worst that could happen anyway? I get what I want?" I proceed to sign the paper and slide it to him across the table. There was a weird noise behind me so I turn around to look, nothing. I turn back around to talk to Lou some more, he's gone. Where did he go? How did he move so fast? Especially without me hearing. This night has been weirder and weirder. I am just going to go home and get some rest. I am sure I will wake up to all of my desires I sarcastically thought. I chuckle to myself while throwing my cup in the trash on the way out. Now I make my way home and when I finally get there, I am beat. I rush to bed without hesitation or doing anything else. I take off my clothes and plop down on my bed and pass out willingly.

I wake, slowly start to open my eyes. Wait, where am I? What is going on here? I seem to be in a big house of some sorts. How did I get here? Don't panic, just get up, get dressed and try to figure out the situation. Alright, leaving the room and walking down the hall. Here is a huge staircase, follow it down. I am sure it leads to the front door. Maybe I can leave without being noticed. I get to the front door and I hear, "Honey, is that you? Don't leave yet I have breakfast for you." A gorgeous brunette comes walking in from what looks like the kitchen. Wow, she's stunning, and she is wearing very small pajamas that doesn't leave much to the imagination.

She says to me, "Well, are you going to just stand there or are you going to come join me for breakfast?"

I respond, "Oh, of course. I don't know what I was thinking. Weird question, or questions. What am I doing here? Who are you?"

"Ha ha, very funny. Like you don't know your own home and your own wife. Get out of here silly."

"Right, ha ha, I was just playing of course."

"Are you going in to the office or just calling to let them know you quit? I am so proud of you for finally doing that. I know you've always wanted to."

"I think I will go in, thanks."

What in the actual fuck is going on? It's almost as if Lou was telling the truth about granting my every desires. Oh my god. He did. Let me check my bank account, twenty million dollars. Holy shit, he did it. How? What? I am so confused. I guess I shouldn't complain, right? I can't believe this is happening. Wait, let me go outside, I do need to go quit my job anyway. Now for the last bit of it, let's see if my car is there! Run back upstairs and let's check out my clothes. Something to wear, something that will make a statement to my boss when I quit. I go into my bedroom and find the closet. Wow, all of these clothes are mine? Holy shit! It's some real fancy stuff I have here, apparently I have really good taste. Just then my wife walks in, she's wearing nothing.

She says to me, "Hey baby, how long do you think you're going to be gone? I don't want to wait too long for you to return. I am not going to put anything on while I wait either."

I reply shakily while looking her up and down, "Really shouldn't take long. I promise I will hurry back as fast as I can. Trust me, I don't want to keep you waiting either."

I need to find Lou; I can't believe that this is really my life now. I run downstairs and go out the front door. I don't think I've ran this fast since running during PE in high school, now I am a little out of breath. Oh my god, there it is. That sixty-nine Pontiac GTO Judge, matte black. Oh shit, I forgot to grab the keys. I run back inside as giddy as a kid in a candy store with twenty dollars. I yell to my wife, "Hunny, do you know where I left my keys to the GTO?" She comes walking down the stairs still in her birthday suit holding them. She doesn't say anything but hands them to me and gives me a big kiss, winks and smacks my ass on the way out the door. Wow, I can get used to this.

I get into my amazing car, sit there and just take in the ambiance. The smell is of old leather. The feel of the steering wheel, everything about it is amazing. Turn the key, the sound of the rumble, the feel of the engine shaking the entire body of the car. The smell of exhaust, but the specific smell only old cars give. How is this real life? Put it into drive, slam on the gas as I peel out of my driveway. Down the street, the menacing sound of my engine roaring like the demon it is. I just realized I have no idea where I am. I pull over and pull out my phone so I can GPS my way to the office. Ok, now I know where to go, wait, pin where I am at so I know how to get back. Slam on the gas again and take off to the office while screaming with joy the whole way.

I arrive safely to the office somehow when I could've been arrested for reckless endangerment for how I was driving. I walk in and walk to my boss's office. He looks at me up and down and says, "Richard, why are you in normal clothes? I heard you didn't show up on time. What is going on?"

I yell back, "I quit mother fucker! I don't give a shit! I made it big time, so fuck you!"

At that moment I walked out of his office without any other explanation. I didn't even look back to see the befuddled look on his face. Now I want to hurry back home and have a great time with my beautiful wife. I wonder if Lou was actually just God in disguise. I still don't understand how he made this happen. Oh well, I hope I can see him one day so I can thank him.

I pull up home, get out of my car and run inside. "Hunny I'm home." I yelled out as soon as I walk in the door.

She yells back, "I am in the living room."

I go through the door where the kitchen is and walk through it to the living room. There she is, sitting, still wearing nothing. I smile really big and then notice that there is someone in the recliner seat. Its Lou, sitting there with that big smile of his.

"Hi Richard. How are you enjoying your most

desired life?" Lou said.

"Hi Lou. I don't know how you did it. This is incredible. How could I ever possibly repay you?" I replied.

"You see, that's the thing, you signed my contract. That means that you will have a year to live to the fullest. After that, things will start to deteriorate. Your wife here, she will cheat on you. In depression you and her will do lots of drugs which will spend all of your money. Then you will have to sell your house and your precious car. Normally people try to fight for longer time in the fun stages but you were so quick to sign I only had to give you a year."

"What, what do you mean? I don't understand. How could this be?" I have a feeling on complete disgust in my stomach.

"Well Richard, that's what happens when you make a deal with the devil. Come on, Samael, Lou, I am Lucifer Morningstar. I am the devil. You really didn't think about my names I gave you? Or how I had you sign something and gave you everything? You might be stupider than I thought. Well, I just wanted to let you know that your year starts today. Enjoy it while it lasts." At that moment he snapped his fingers while laughing and disappeared.

In shock I look around, what did I get myself into? Holy shit, how am I going to live my life knowing that in a year everything is going to come crashing down? What the fuck do I do? Oh my God, why is this happening to me? I look up and my wife looks at me and says, "Hey, where did Lou go? He was telling me a cool story. Oh well, want to meet me upstairs now?" She smiles **really** big and runs upstairs. What the fuck did I do? I guess when they say things are too good to be true, it really is. I walk over to the kitchen, open up the drawer and grab a kitchen knife. I proceed to slit my wrists. I whisper out loud as I bleed out on my kitchen floor, "See you in hell Lou. I won't give you the pleasure of watching me suffer for a year knowing it will go to shit anyway."

About the Author

Mike Gregory is a first time author. He grew up in a small city in Southern California called Glendora. As a child he grew up loving all things scary, paranormal, or different from the norm. It all started with watching horror movies and reading Goosebumps as a young child. His childhood house was haunted, in which many of his friends had experienced wild things that had happened at his house. He grew up with a single Mother and one sister. Mike met his wife Linda at a young age in which they are still together with three children. If you would like to get to know him better you can find him on Twitter/Instagram/Tik Tok under the handle @mikegreg85. *Please add a short review on Amazon and let me know what you thought!*

Go to the site below to find an easy access to all my links.

www.beacons.ai/mikegregory

CPSIA information can be obtained
at www.ICGtesting.com
Printed in the USA
LVHW040519060423
743575LV00004B/886